THE OLD IRVING PARK LITERARY SOCIETY

THE OLD IRVING PARK LITERARY SOCIETY

PETER M. KATSAROS

BERWICK COURT PUBLISHING CO.
CHICAGO, IL

Peter M. Katsaros is a nationally-known trial lawyer, law professor, public speaking consultant, and man of letters.

Berwick Court Publishing Company
Chicago, Illinois
http://www.berwickcourt.com

Cover design by Steve Dennis

Library of Congress Control Number: 2012901425

ISBN: 978-0-9838846-0-6

Printed in the United States of America

Dedication

To Beth, for a marriage made in heaven and for the extraordinary gifts of our handsome, talented children; my lovely partner Joanne, the most generous person I know; Sarah, Steve and Molly; Matt and Stacey, Patrick, Charley, and Jack; Kathryn and Burke; Chris and Emily and the community of saints who loved my family so well all these years. You know who you are. I am deeply grateful to all of you.

Author's Notes

The fictional pieces in this book are just that: fiction. They are intended to be satire. They were inspired by news in Chicago—the city I love, and news in the U.S.A.—the country I love, that the Republican Party is trying mightily to ruin. These stories should never be read as reporting events that actually occurred or describing people that really lived in our modern times. These events and people exist only in my imagination. I have had such a wonderful life there.

NOM DE PLUME

As he was working on this book, my publisher, a bright young lawyer named Matt Balson, told me that I should tell the readers about my use of the pen name Voltaire. I am not sure I should. Mark Twain didn't explain his choice of a pen name.

Academics are still musing about whether Sam Clemens' nom de plume came from his Mississippi river boating days or his many drunken episodes as a miner, roustabout, and young journalist out West.

Perhaps a middle ground will do. I admire Voltaire for many reasons including leading the Enlightenment; his brilliance as a philosopher, dramatist and satirist; his ecumenical faith; his courage; his tolerance; his generosity and his zest for life.

There you go Matt. Now get off my back and go sell this book widely.

Contents

Contents (cont'd)

Preface: Finding the Muse

My creative writing started five years ago when a friend and I ambled down to the Newberry Library in Chicago to take a course on Writing Short Shorts. The course lasted eight weeks and met on a weekday evening for a couple of hours.

Brooke Bergan, a long time Newberry prof and poet, taught the course to about a dozen writers. Brooke was a maverick. What poet isn't, you ask. She was lively, friendly and kind.

After the introductions of the writers and a vignette about her casting off her nineteen-year-old boyfriend (Brooke was in her fifties), she said that her job was to "give us assignments." I think I heard that after I ordered my imagination back from its sprint into speculation about the prof's love life.

Brooke's writing deadlines worked beautifully for me. Perhaps the deadlines were a catalyst for all the years of rich, exciting schooling and fine mentors that I have had. Perhaps the deadlines allured me to express the great happiness that I have had in my life. Or, maybe the admiration I have for the deft writing style of one fine writer after another burst out.

I am not sure what it was but my writing in June 2005 took off, like my young buddy Finn White would say, "like a rocket."

Brooke gave me an assignment and a deadline to bring in

something new every week and I, the dutiful student, snapped to attention to put some pent-up stories and my soul down on paper. I loved the writing life.

I love watching language, good ideas and vivid scenes finding a home on clean white pages. I love hearing good language from leaders, poets, a playwright as brilliant and bold as Mamet, and a Greek as wise and earthy as Harry Mark Petrakis.

What is even more fun is seeing the writing entertain my loved ones and friends, bringing them laughter and, as Garrison Keillor said of good poets, "giving hope some feathers."

Writing came easily each week of Brooke's class. It didn't matter if the assigned work was an essay, short fiction, a poem or dialogue for a play. The words jumped up on that computer screen like water over a dam. I *heard* the words first, very clearly, and soon they were in print.

Writing is exciting. All creative work is exciting. I encourage everyone to write, believe in yourself, and then write some more. I want to hear what you have to say about life. I want you to share your wisdom with me and my family and friends.

Get on with it. I will brook no excuses.

I remember my joy after graduating college, and finding that I finally had no limits on my time to read anything I wanted. I had been a hell of a college student, studying night, day, and weekends for four years to keep my academic scholarship and be welcomed into the finest law schools in the country. But, that dedication to the study of constitutional and labor law left no time for creative writing and the humanities.

I have vivid memories of a Christmas break during my junior year in college when I devoured Twain's "Connecticut Yankee in King Arthur's Court." I traveled right back into those medieval times as rapidly as the Yankee had been shell-shocked into his adventures. I was happily lost in the story and in Twain's satire.

Fortunately, I have had the time and the resources to pursue an insatiable curiosity for America's finest journalists, trial lawyers, novelists, historians, playwrights and poets.

I live in an old Victorian house (1875) in Chicago with a huge library that my wife and I built up over the years. Many happy hours have been spent in that room on the fainting couch with the novels of Raymond Chandler, Dashiell Hammett, James Ellroy and biographies of FDR, Lincoln, Churchill, Mark Twain, Shakespeare, A.J. Liebling and most recently Voltaire, the star of the Enlightenment.

While the library has been one of my favorite rooms in the house, once I took up creative writing I christened our office in the house "The Writing Room." That is where many of the pieces in this collection were born.

The library in this room includes the books closest to my heart: my spiritual favorites by Jack Shea, Joseph Campbell and Anna Quindlen; the creative writing coaches led by Brenda Ueland, William Blake, Jane Cameron and Ray Bradbury; the Greek mythology collections, some illustrated and some not, and encyclopedias of literature.

My writing has taken over the house, you might say. Some of the essays that follow have been written on the front porch of the house. An extraordinarily sunny place ringed with windows that allow me to watch mothers, their children, and dozens of devoted dog-lovers out of the corner of my eye, this porch is a serene place for the imagination to run long.

I am grateful to Brooke Bergan, to my dear friends and family, and to the wonderful writers that have thrilled me since childhood.

Hope you all find time for *your* writing. The world will be a better place for us if you do.

STORIES

Mr. Katsaros (left) and Dr. Martinez (right), leaders of the Old Irving Park Literary Society

Chapter One: The Old Irving Park Literary Society

The Old Irving Park Literary Society is the oldest and most exclusive of its kind in the United States. It was formed by Lord Byron, the famous British romantic writer, and James Russell Lowell, the American satirist, abolitionist and man of letters.

The society was formed to foster the advancement of the arts and humanities through the publication of the most visionary writers, philosophers and spiritual teachers.

An invitation to join the Society guarantees the member fame, fortune and a front seat in the literary world.

The society is now headquartered in Chicago, Illinois and is led by Dr. Charles Martinez, a physician and writer, and Mr. Peter Katsaros, a trial lawyer, dramatist and writer.

Dr. Martinez and Mr. Katsaros, due to the fame that comes with leading the Society, are always accompanied by bodyguards. Without them neither man would make it to work without the constant entreaties by writers and artists for attention to their applications for membership in the Society. Dr. Martinez also travels with his wife, Monica, his young beagle, Jakers, and his granddaughters Phoebe and Tessa (both of whom have serious literary talent and are beautiful, energetic girls).

The Martinez and Katsaros homes face each other on Byron

street in Chicago, a stone's throw away from other lovely Victorian houses on Lowell Avenue in the Old Irving Park neighborhood. That proximity of the leaders of the Society makes it easier to administer as well as tend to each others cars when vicious Chicago winters encase them in ice or overwhelm the last breaths of their batteries.

The last American admitted to the Society was Garrison Keillor. Keillor has an extraordinary range as a writer and humorist. He runs effortlessly down the roads of music, fiction, dramatic essay, theatre and spirituality. In Mr. Katsaros' opinion Keillor is Mark Twain with a healthy soul.

Keillor's election to the Society was rather easy. Both directors found him to be a master storyteller with an inexhaustible supply of wit, wisdom and hope for all of us. Dr. Martinez found Keillor's singing voice a bit distracting but nothing that three years of voice lessons in Vienna could not cure.

Upon Keillor's election to the Society he invited the two Directors to join him on his weekly radio show. The Directors leapt at the idea. Dr. Martinez offered to play a role in a Dusty and Lefty skit, while Mr. Katsaros chose a role in the ongoing series Guy Noir, Private Eye. That episode of the show won dozens of radio awards. The Directors are considering offers to become regulars.

One of the applicants now under review is Anna Quindlen, the essayist and novelist. Quindlen is a gifted writer with a beautiful soul. She is fearless in telling her fellow Americans to slow down and appreciate the beauty and abundance in their lives. Mr. Katsaros is a strong proponent of Quindlen's admission. Dr. Martinez is studying her work now before he casts his vote. His review has been interrupted by his golf game, the editing of his memoir and the writing of some clever, funny short stories about the many characters he met growing up. Ms. Quindlen is desperate for an answer, but like thousands of others—and for those negotiating life in general—patience is needed.

Ernest Hemingway was rejected for membership in a close vote—Dr.. Martinez voting for admission and Mr. Katsaros voting against. (Admission to the Society must be by unanimous vote). Mr. Katsaros reasoned that no one should be in the Society whose writing so depressed him that he took his own life. Dr. Martinez said that if depression was a disqualification, thousands of fine writers would be disqualified. Mr. Katsaros was amused but unmoved.

Sinclair Lewis was accepted into membership in the Society after a ferocious debate that almost required the intervention of a priest. However, no sober priest could be found at the time, so the directors worked it out on their own.

Mr. Katsaros was a fierce proponent of Sinclair Lewis,. Having read most of his captivating novels, Mr. Katsaros both understood and seconded Lewis' view of the rapaciousness of unbridled American capitalism. Dr. Martinez ("Chuckie" to only his closest friends), who secretly believes that Lewis was a Communist, opposed the admission of Lewis because Lewis grew up in a small town in Minnesota and because his novels can be ponderous, lacking in any gun-toting desperadoes.

The Lewis nomination was tabled for several years until the Lewis Estate could come up with an extra $20,000 to add to the $10,000 application fee. After that, the nomination sailed through. This is Chicago, you know.

Chapter Two: The Spirit of Mike Royko

He slouched in a beautifully appointed library in a Victorian home on the Near North side of heaven. Floor to ceiling mahogany bookcases had a topical arrangement – politics, law, biographies and spirituality on the left; literature, poetry and children's books on the right. A baby grand piano in the corner sat atop the parquet floor, facing a marble fireplace.

The Spirit of Mike Royko sat in a chair in the library drinking his first cup of morning coffee and stared into a huge gilt-edged mirror above the fireplace mantel. He wore jeans, a Chicago Daily News softball team T-shirt and dirty sneakers.

Mike was grumbling to himself again, this time more desperately than ever before.

"I have got to get the hell out of here and back to Chicago. People are just too nice here. There is no action, no conflict, and besides the point, people in Chicago are suffering. I have to get out and there is only one way to do it – by talking the big GAL into it. I am bored with bliss and I miss my family."

Mike was startled by several knocks on the library door, followed by the delicious lilting giggles of little children. GOD entered the library with three small children tugging at her maroon robe. She sat down in a chair opposite Mike with her three children on her lap. "Good morning Mike. I heard from

St. Peter that you had a problem and wanted to talk. How can I help?" She hugged her children closely and looked kindly at Royko.

"Thanks for coming, God. Your children are beautiful. I am told that you and St. Peter have been married over two thousand years. What a wonderful life that must have been. I am not much for going to church but I do think that the churches got it right when they made marriage a sacrament."

"I agree with you. You were married, weren't you?"

"Yes, I was. Twice. Two fine women–finer than me. I met Carol before I went into the service and courted her in my own awkward way since I was a kid. She was gorgeous. I was crazy about her–wrote her a lot of love letters, probably my best writing. We married and had two sons. Then, I started screwing up–became a workaholic and an alcoholic, all at the same time. Neglected my kids *and* Carol in hot pursuit of fame and fortune.

"Then, I learned something–the hard way of course. I was never too bright. Yeah, I could turn a phrase or two, but a genius I am not. You see, Carol died young, on my forty-seventh birthday. I guess you can understand why I have never celebrated a birthday since."

God shifted a bit in her chair, as her children started to nod off to sleep. "I am so sorry that that happened. What did you do, then?"

"My reaction? Drink more, take time off from writing and feel sorry for myself. None of that was good for me, but as I told you God, I am not a smart guy, just a smart aleck.

"Well, I finally pulled myself together with the help of my family and friends. I returned to writing and was lucky enough to marry another lovely woman, Judy. Judy worked for the paper and had been an outstanding tennis player and coach. We started a family together and with her help, I finally got the alcohol problem under control. We were having a fine time of it—even though I did have to compromise many of my principles by working for the *Chicago Tribune*. Now, that is one of those mortal sins, for which no one should be forgiven."

"So, what brought you here?"

"As I was saying, Judy and I were sailing through life and headed right into another storm—the storm that got me here. I had that fatal stroke that took me from my family and my writing when I was sixty two.

"I had finally figured out how to live the good life. My golf game was just getting respectable and BAM! I find myself up here golfing with St. Andrew, A.J. Liebling, Mark Twain and Edward R. Murrow.

"Now, don't get me wrong, God. These guys are fine, but Jeeesus, is A.J. fat! Great writer and all, but he really slows down the game."

God spoke up. "Mike, my kids are a getting restless. Peter and I promised to take them to the beach this morning. So, I must be going in a little while. Please tell me what troubles you."

"Well, God......I want to......go back to Chicago......for a little while. One of my sons is in real trouble and the City of Chicago is in trouble too. One of my older sons—one of the two I had with Carol and neglected—pled guilty to a crime recently. I have to help him recover. I guess I want to be the father to him that I should have been a long time ago.

"And then there is a second reason. Chicagoans are suffering from an epidemic of suicides. Almost weekly, a Chicagoan leaps off the Michigan Avenue Bridge into the Chicago River.

Death is almost instantaneous. Not from the pollution as you might expect but from the impact of the fall. The suicide notes are alarmingly similar. They all are in despair from having to read the *Trib*'s replacement for me–some dude named Fass or Brass or Kass–I am not sure of the name except that it rhymes with ass.

"So, I am asking you for permission to go back to Chicago to help my son and to help the City by writing a few more columns.

"Will you allow me to go.........just for a little while?"

God thought for a moment and then said, "Mike, I am sorry, but I don't think I can let you go back. I sent my eldest son down there and, as you know, it turned out rather badly. Were you to go back, there would be even more confusion among the faithful.

"I assure you that I will always give my people hope and hopeful messages every day. Whether they are awake enough to hear these messages is another problem entirely.

"As for you, I don't think I could answer your request to return home any more eloquently than to repeat the words you used on the passing of the Chicago Daily News. You wrote: 'When I was a kid, the worst of all days was the last day of summer vacation, and we were in the schoolyard playing softball, and the sun was down and it was getting dark. I didn't want the game to end. It was too good, too much fun. I wanted it to stay light forever, so we could go on playing forever, so the game would go on and on.

'That's how I feel now. C'mon, c'mon. Let's play one more inning. One more time at bat. One more pitch. Just one? Stick around, guys. We can't break up this team. It's too much fun.

'But the sun always went down. And now it's almost dark again.'"

God rose abruptly from her chair, gave Mike a warm embrace and then scooped up her children as she strode confidently out of the library.

Mike sat back in his chair and wept long and hard.

* * * *

Author's Comments:

I love this piece. Reading it still makes me laugh. I hope it works for you, too.

The themes in this piece have evolved from this learning in my life: tolerance should be at the heart of any faith. Just read Voltaire, Joseph Campbell or any other enlightened theologian or poet. Humanity advances when tolerance is shown.

Marriage is a sacrament in some faiths for good reasons. I had the gift of that Sacrament for almost twenty-five years until the death of my wife in 2001. What a wonderful comforting gift my marriage was.

God is a woman. She must be. Women take much better care of each other than men do and are less likely to engage in "disposable relationships." That is a fact.

Chicago journalism is in very bad shape today and has been declining in quality for decades. The papers are struggling because of their poor quality and not just because of ad revenue lost to the Internet. Investigative journalism in Chicago is dead. The only time an investigative story is broken in our fair city is when the U.S. Attorney indicts someone. Corruption is rampant in this town.

What a gifted writer, satirist, and humorist Mike Royko was over a forty-year career and eight thousand columns. What joy and laughter he brought to Chicago. I have studied and admired his writing for many years and often pull down an anthology of his writing from my library shelves to study his style and to laugh again.

Just imagine the guts he had to challenge the elder Daley and his thousands of lieutenants.

Alcoholism contributed to Royko's early death at 62. The drinking and accompanying workaholism contributed to the problems plaguing one of his sons.

I wish you all the best in avoiding both addictions.

Chapter Three: Ubi Est Mia?

Chicago in the 21st century. You can say a lot of things about Chicago—some good and some bad—but one thing that all Americans can agree upon is that Chicagoans know how politics works.

We know that things happen in politics—local and national—when money changes hands.

In the last thirty-five years, the U.S. Attorney's office in Chicago has been working round the clock shifts convicting corrupt politicians, city and state employees, judges and two former Governors and their kitchen cabinet of taking bribes.

Our beloved and greatly missed dean of Chicago journalism, Mike Royko, wrote the political primer for Chicagoans in his eight thousand columns. In a 1967 column, Mike suggested changing the city's motto from *Urbs in Horto* (City in a Garden) to *Ubi Est Mea* (Where's Mine?).

Given our city's steady diet of rampant political corruption, it was to be expected that politics would be kicked around when my buddies and I met for coffee at the Dunkin' Donuts shop at Diversey and Halsted.

Ed, scanning the front page of the *New York Times*, choked on his coffee as he read the news that a Texas lawyer shot in the face and chest by Vice President Dick Chainy had just apologized to the Veep for causing him so much embarrassment. "Holy Christ, I cannot believe this," Ed screamed, once the pain of the scorching coffee had passed. "This joker gets blown away and almost killed by that big Dick and now he's apologizing. What's wrong with this picture?"

The rest of us nodded in disbelief. Joe said: "It makes perfect sense. Harry Half-Wittington was paid off. A well-educated, clout-heavy lawyer wouldn't say anything that stupid unless he has been threatened or bribed. Or both."

Being the writer in the group, I volunteered to do some digging to see if Joe was right. I called a couple of other writers, Pam Nolan and Lisa Day, and we went to work. A couple of weeks later, I returned with the story.

"Okay, this is what Pam, Lisa and I dug up. Joe was right. Money changed hands and a threat had been made."

And I laid it out for them.

* * * *

A couple of days after Harry Half-Wittington had been shot, he called Dan Webbster, a Chicago trial lawyer in a Republican firm in the Loop. In the first call to Webbster, Harry spoke in a raspy and faint voice: "Dan, this is Harry down in Corpus Christi. I need some advice and I need it now. Will you help me?"

Dan tensed up and turned his swivel chair to look out his bay window at Monroe Harbor. The aqua lakefront glistened. "Harry, you sound terrible. What happened?"

"That big Dick shot me in the face!"

"Which big Dick?"

"Chainy."

"Holy Christ! How?"

"He was bombed and full of his heart meds. He insisted on going out for quail, so we tagged along. I downed a few birds and went over to pick them up. As I came back, he shot me! I just got out of intensive care. I have 200 pellets in me and one of them has traveled to my heart."

"I am so sorry. What are your doctors saying?"

"Uncertain. We just don't know. Listen, Dan—I am very scared. Very, very scared."

"I am sure you are; you were nearly killed."

"That's not the whole of it, Dan. It's the threats."

"What threats?"

"Scooter."

"Scooter?"

"Yes. I was just coming out of intensive care. I hadn't even seen my family yet. I woke up and there was Scooter sitting at my bedside, reading a Bible tucked inside the magazine, *Bust*. As soon as I was able to speak, he got up, stood over my bed and told me that I had better play ball with Chainy. I was told to do exactly what Chainy told me to do. Otherwise, they would bust me real badly and I would wind up sleeping in a tent outside W's ranch next to Cindy Sheehan. I was so scared that I passed out. As soon as I came to, I called you. What the hell do I do?"

Webbster reacted quickly. "First, let me worry about the threats. You just rest and do what the doctors say. I'll call you back shortly with a strategy. Got that?"

"Absolutely. Will you be able to help?"

"Harry, I'm from Chicago. Politics is in our drinking water. Hardball politics is our game. I will figure this one out."

"That's why I called you. Many thanks."

****

Ed and Joe were enthralled—so much so that their coffee had gone untouched. Neither was at all surprised by the real, untold story. Both of them had spent seven years in the Jesuit order, followed by decades of Alinski-inspired community organizing in Chicago. Plenty of political sophistication in those two guys.

I continued the story.

****

Webbster took out a legal pad and a calculator. He made a few notes, tapped a few keys and smiled his biggest smile. Then he called the firm's Managing Partner—Big Jim Thompson—for a meeting.

He led off the meeting telling Big Jim the full account of Harry's call and that he wanted to take Harry's personal injury case against Chainy.

Big Jim leapt out of his chair. "No fucking way. Are you crazy? Chainy and his thugs will kill you and me *and* this law firm. And let's not forget, Dan, that you are not having a very good year here. You just blew 20 million dollars in fees defending George "I Don't Need a Checkbook" Ryan in a losing cause. Dan, what you need to do is bring in good, paying work and lots of it. Go out there and bring in more of those tobacco companies you've been defending. That's the kind of work we need."

Webbster shook his head. "Jim, you missed the point. We

can earn three million dollars for the firm in this case in a week or less. We can recoup some of the loss we took on the Ryan case and put a million in profit away by March 15th. Not a bad month, wouldn't you say?"

"I get it, Dan. Can you pull it off?"

"Sure. I'll just hold a private negotiation with Scooter. We can do it in a few phone calls and then make the settlement confidential."

After getting Half-Wittington's approval, Webbster called Scooter and opened the negotiation. "Scooter, I talked it over at length with Harry and we have decided to demand nine million to settle the case with Chainy."

"Nine million! For what? That's outrageous!"

"Scooter, let's not waste time in posturing. I am going to give it to you straight. Chainy was blind drunk when he shot Harry. We both know that hunting rules say that you do not shoot unless you know where everyone in your hunting party is. Harry was wearing bright orange hunting clothes. Need I say one word more?"

Scooter grunted. "You trial lawyers disgust me. You're all bottom-feeders."

"Scooter, let's not make this personal. This is business. Strictly business. Chainy is lucky I'm a Republican. The price would be one hell of a lot higher with a Democratic firm. So, do we have a deal?"

"We'll take the deal as long as it's confidential and Harry makes a public apology to Chainy for the embarrassment stemming from the accident."

"I will recommend that to Harry. Hell, I'd tell him to say that Chainy's the greatest prophet since Isaiah, if he pays the money. I'll call Harry and get this deal in motion."

Webbster hung up with Libby and quickly called Harry at the hospital. "Harry, this is Dan. I got you a great deal—a cool nine million. Six for you, three for us."

Harry paused and asked, "What conditions are there?"

"Nothing major—confidentiality and you have to say something stupid in public when you leave the hospital."

"How stupid?"

"Incredibly stupid. Something like, 'This past weekend encompassed all of us in a cloud of misfortune and sadness that is not easy to explain, especially to those who are not familiar with the great sport of quail hunting. My family and I are deeply sorry for all that Vice President Chainy and his family have had to go through this past week.'"

"Oh my God. How can I say that with a straight face?"

"Harry, if you can't say it, have somebody else in the family say it for you. Or one of your docs, for that matter. Nine million, remember?"

"Okay, Dan."

So, the deal was done. A pile of money changed hands. Half-Wittington made the public apology that even Slats Grobnik and Wanda knew was nonsense.

****

My buddies and I pondered another day of public corruption.

Joe beamed with pride for having explained presciently Half-Wittington's absurd public remarks upon leaving the hospital. Ed turned to me and asked how the story had been found.

I quickly answered: "I have a source in W's Permanent

Office for Wiretapping Innocent Americans. With some coaxing, I got transcripts of all of Harry's phone calls since the shooting occurred."

The Chicagoans sat back, grinning.

Chapter Four:
The Mayor and the Law

St. Peter awoke suddenly from a brief nap. He was laying on the fainting couch in his library, a Victorian-styled room with a baby grand piano in the northeast corner and dark mahogany bookcases encircling the room, brimming with the wisdom of the ages.

A brown red-rope file had fallen off St. Peter's lap as he slept, spilling its half-dozen Petitions for Admission to Heaven onto the Oriental rug beneath him. As St. Peter gathered up the papers and stuffed them back into the file, there was a loud knock at the library door.

"Who's there?" St. Peter grumbled, clearing some phlegm from his throat.

"It's Mike Royko, may I come in?"

"Of course, Mike. Come on in and let's talk awhile."

Royko walked in wearing a Chicago Daily News T-shirt, dirty and sweat-stained from a softball game he had finished minutes ago. He took in the rich tapestry of St. Peter's library and summoned up the chutzpah for his plea.

"Uhhh, St. Peter, don't get me wrong on this, but I am here to ask for a leave to go back to Chicago for a while to help some folks that are kinda desperate."

"What do you mean desperate?"

"I mean Chicagoans have been losing hope since I died and my political column ceased. My people are so distraught at the journalistic gruel being fed them by the *Tribune* and the *Sun-Times*, that they have been driven to despair, some to suicide!"

"Suicide, Mike? Surely, you jest."

"Unfortunately, St. Peter, it is the truth."

"Oh, dear dear, this is serious. How long will you be gone?"

"With your permission, I think I can rattle off a few columns, lift their spirits, and be back in a week."

"Then, by all means, go, and Godspeed to you. Just make sure you email me your columns. I was a big fan of yours for years."

"Thanks, so much, St. Peter. There is so much to be done in giving people hope."

Having received the blessing of St. Peter, Royko nabbed the last seat in first class on the Angelic Express. The plane touched down at O'Hare just after five in the evening. Royko wore a New York Yankees baseball cap and Perry Ellis sunglasses as he exited the flight, trying to be inconspicuous. He devoured an issue of The Nation and The New Yorker for the cutting-edge journalism that he loved so dearly.

The first decision he faced was where to do his writing. Should he return to the *Chicago Tribune* for a day? Royko thought not. The *Trib* was home to right-wing ideologues like John Kass and the editorial board that had endorsed the drunken, frat boy, war-monger for re-election in 2004. That did it for Mike.

Royko recalled fondly the day he quit the *Chicago Sun-Times* in 1983, which just so happened to be the day that yellow journalist Rupert Murdoch took over control of it. At his dramatic exit and press conference, Royko had said: "No self-respecting fish would want to be wrapped in Murdoch's publications. He puts out trash." The *Trib* had earned the same rebuff.

Royko had to think of a plan and quickly, before someone else took a header off the bridge. Blasting though the dizzying effects of the three strong gin and tonics that he had inhaled on the flight, Royko knew where he could write—the backroom of Sam Sianis' Billy Goat Tap near Michigan and Grand. He'd worry about a publisher later.

Royko grabbed a cab to the Billy Goat, got a warm greeting and hug from Sam, and was ushered to a back office reeking of the grease from the hundreds of thousands of cheeseburgers sold there since the 1940's. Royko calmed down, felt the warmth of Chicago hugging him and then dashed off this scene.

* * * *

(July 22, 2005, 5th floor of City Hall, the Mayor seated at his desk at ten in the morning, scowling).

Mayor: Mary Margaret, get the hell in here, we have work to do!

Mary Margaret Callahan Moran, the Mayor's 87-year-old secretary, jumped out of her chair and walked quickly toward the Mayor's office. Remembering the scolding that she received a week ago for clutching her rosary in the Mayor's presence, she threw it into her bodice, giving her dress the first shapeliness it had ever had. She rather liked it.

Mayor: Get my car ready right away. I have a meeting with

the Cardinal down in Bridgeport.

Mary Margaret: Yessir.

Daley's limousine streaked down Clark Street, through Chinatown and into Bridgeport, pulling to a stop in front of his old church, Our Lady of Perpetual Hope. Daley jumped out, bounded up the steps, crossed himself three times and slipped into the third confessional. On the other side of the screen sat Cardinal Bernard Law, the former Cardinal of the Catholic Archdiocese of Boston, now a high-ranking prelate in the Vatican.

Mayor: Father, thank you so much for hearing my confession. You have come a long way to help.

Law: My son, we are happy to help in anyway we can. I thought that the confessional gave you the best legal protection for our talk.

Mayor: I totally agree.

Law: So, how can I help?

Mayor: Father, I am in trouble. The last year has been nothing but a series of scandals in city government being exposed by both the press and that damn trial lawyer, Patrick Fitzgerald in the U.S. Attorney's Office. That guy is fearless. He is breathing down the necks of Karl Rove *and* me, both at the same time. I think he just wants to be Governor of Illinois. I just don't know what to do.

Law: Not to worry, Mr. Mayor. I have been through years and years of pedophile scandals and scores of lawsuits in Boston, and thank God, we have weathered the storm. I came out smelling like a rose with a brand new job, great digs and a promotion. My office is right down the hall from the Holy See.

Mayor: Holy See? Who's that?

Law: Pope Benedict. Didn't you go to Catholic school?

Mayor: I did but I failed the confirmation test twice, just like the Illinois Bar Exam. So, how did you get through all the scandals?

Law: Two ways. First, I took a long sabbatical to Michigan for some rest and golf, during which I settled all the lawsuits against the Archdiocese for a hefty sum. After that, I kept a low profile until the public controversy died down and my promotion came through. With the unflagging support of the Vatican, we basically blew off all those American Catholics so upset about my conduct and then went about our business as usual. You must have seen me officiating at one of the funeral masses held before the burial of Pope John Paul.

Mayor: Come to think of it, Maggie mentioned you to me that week. She saw you on TV.

Law: Think about it. Take your family up to your compound in Michigan for some R&R. It's the summertime. Nobody will blame you for some time off. The lawsuits will take years to resolve. The public's memory is really, really short. You have good relations with the *Trib* and the *Sun-Times*. Serious, investigative journalism is dead in Chicago, anyway. It died when Royko stopped doing it in the 70's. Keep wining and dining The *Trib* and Hollinger, working with them, doing some civil service reform (nothing too serious, you know), and six months from now, your public approval rankings will be back in the 70th percentile.

Mayor: Great ideas, all of them. Thanks so much, Father.

Law: You are welcome, my son. Peace be with you.

(The screen between Law and the Mayor was lifted and the Cardinal put a piece of paper into the Mayor's hand. The Mayor strained to read the paper in the dim light of the confessional. He finally made

out the Vatican Crest, followed by the words: Invoice for professional services– $15,000).

Mayor: Cardinal, since when did you start charging for confessions?

Law: Mr. Mayor, church revenues are way down this year because of all those pesky trial lawyers. We all have to adapt to change, don't we?

Mayor: I guess so, Father. Again, thanks and peace be with you. Congratulations on the promotion.

(With that the Mayor took his limousine straight home, packed up his family and headed for the Daley compound in Michigan for an extended vacation).

* * * *

Back in the bar, Mike Royko thanked his confidential source for coverage of Daley in the confessional, grabbed the last seat on the Angelic Express for heaven and got out of town and beyond the jurisdiction of a subpoena from U.S. Attorney Patrick Fitzgerald.

Royko's piece appeared in the Chicago Reader as the front page story and the Michigan Avenue suicides ceased immediately. St. Peter was delighted with the developments.

* * * *

Author's Comments:

It pays to read the New York Times as often as you can. Once the Times gets into a story, fine research is published. Cardinal Bernard Law's trouble in Boston was covered in detail for years.

My dear friend Jim Sherman played Cardinal Law in "Sin," a riveting play about Law and his problems as the Roman Catholic Cardinal in Boston when the pedophilia scandal broke. Jim won a Jeff award for his acting in a show put on by Bailiwick Theatre in Chicago. I never thought I could muster an ounce of sympathy for Law until I saw Jim's portrayal of Law's struggle.

Saturday mornings usually give me more time with the Times. I remember choking on my coffee when I read about Law getting a top job at the Vatican and handling one of the key Masses prior to the funeral of the Pope John Paul. Law's Vatican job inexplicably followed the Boston scandal.

Richard M. Daley, a resilient politician and good city manager, did indeed survive the political challenges described in the story and won re-election by a huge margin. Chicago may be ready for reform but...perhaps not right away.

Chapter Five: My Trade is to Say What I Think

I spent a wonderful long life writing satire in the form of poems, plays and in my distinct creation–the philosophical tales.

What great fun that writing was: 20,000 letters and 100 books. I still laugh for hours when I reread Candide. I am so deeply grateful to Leonard Bernstein for writing the music that brought this, my favorite creation, back onto the world stage in the 20th century.

Yes, I admit I caught quite a bit of hell for my writing. Two trips to the Bastille before I turned thirty and a violent mugging by a gang hired by an aristocrat I had offended convinced me that France in the early 18th century was no place for freedom of thought, nor my unconventional pen.

England was a far better place. I loved the intellectual freedom of England during my three years there after my ouster from France. I even wrote a book about my learning there, *Letters on the English.*

You know much of the rest of my story. Most of my books had to be smuggled into Paris and sold underground. Read my *Philosophical Dictionary* and you will see why. Both the hateful, fearful Catholic Church and the French Regent had the ear of the French prosecutor, so returning to France was not possible. I instead made my home in Ferney in Switzerland. I did my best to make that home the intellectual capital of Europe in the Enlightenment. Quite a few historians say I did a good job at it.

Ferney was a delightful place. Plenty of space, beautiful gardens, a great library, and guest quarters for visiting thinkers from all over Europe who wanted to come and study and talk a while. I built a church on the grounds and hired a priest I could tolerate. Life was very, very good.

And, do you know what ? I returned to Paris a hero on the eve of my death in 1778. The prayer that I had always lofted skyward was ringing in my ears. "God, may you reveal all my enemies to be wholly ridiculous." God had answered me.

I led a life dedicated to truth, beauty, tolerance and justice. Such a life carries risks, but they are all worth it.

– Voltaire

Chapter Six: Abbott Joseph Liebling

I met the most fascinating man the other day after returning from a four mile run in a fresh snowfall near the Bahai temple: the very, very rotund and brilliant Renaissance man, A. J. Liebling.

I met the owlish Joe Liebling (as he insisted I call him) outside a Greek coffee house in my neighborhood. He was sitting at two tables pushed together and strewn with newspapers. I was attracted to him by his mumbling and cursing to himself about bad writing and publishers and all sorts of sins of the Fourth Estate in America.

Sidling up to him I hoped he would have time for some good rich talk. Talk as dark and delicious as the first cup of fresh coffee in the morning. Fortunately, I found him to be a warm, amiable man with an intellect as thirsty and insatiable as mine.

Over the next four hours I learned about Liebling's exciting career as a writer for *The New Yorker*. Writing for that fine publication from 1935 until his early death in 1963, this Francophile wrote masterful and ground-breaking press criticism, sports reporting about the boxing scene in New York, war reporting from Europe during World War II, as well as French gourmet cooking reviews. An impressive breadth of knowledge.

Anyone interested in a career as a writer should study Joe's use of the English language. Writers can feast endlessly on his work and wisdom.

I have read some of Joe's wonderful press criticism in his essays in *The Wayward Pressman* and *The Press*. My American correspondent Peter Katsaros tells me that these books are a must read for every American citizen. Peter added that reading Liebling's books on the press in his law school days was the high point. Who am I to disagree?

Had Liebling lived in my day he would have been a frequent visitor to Cirey and Ferney, my homes. Joe wrote with a joyful and honest pen. America is lucky to have had him write for the ages.

And I am thrilled to have him as a new friend.

– Voltaire

Chapter Seven: Royko and Liebling at the Newseum

Joe Liebling and I have been hanging around since I met him last week at the coffee house. I have been having a lovely time of it as he has told me many stories about his career in journalism in America. He had a thrilling forty-year career. Few writers do.

Joe spent a fair amount of time in my beloved France during the dark days of World War II. In more peaceful days after the War ended, Joe wrote columns about the joy of French cooking. Gargantuan French meals were the mainstay for Joe at that time, undoubtedly leading to his gout and hastening his death at a mere 62 years of age.

I was walking by the Greek coffee house last Friday with Joe when we came upon a tall grumpy man swearing as he leafed through some Chicago newspapers. Joe knew him and introduced me to Mike Royko.

Mike had a firm handshake, which I was soon to learn had developed from a lifetime of playing Chicago softball and thousands of rounds of golf.

I, the curious one, asked Mike what was troubling him so. He said, "The goddamn Chicago newspapers are in the toilet. I knew this was going to happen. It started with Murdoch, continued with Conrad Black. Awful. I am sick. I need a drink."

Joe said, "Mike, what you don't need is another drink. It is your drinking and my reckless eating that got us to heaven ahead of our contemporaries."

I thought about having met two American writers in the past week, both of whom were so upset over the state of journalism in America. I ventured forth boldly (I know no other way) with a suggestion.

"I have an idea. Let's take a trip to America and get a closer view of what's going on in journalism. Where should we go?"

Mike said, "Chicago. It desperately needs us. Chicagoans are so distressed with the *Chicago Tribune* and the *Chicago Sun-Times* that they are regularly diving off the Michigan Avenue bridge to their death in the Chicago River."

Joe responded, "Mike, that is tragic but New York is the place. Home to my beloved *The New Yorker* and *The New York Times*."

"The *New York Times* that missed the absurdity of Bush's Iraq War. That *New York Times* ?"

A storm was brewing. Royko appeared volatile and likely to throw a punch at the portly Liebling. Joe had never seen a punch up close and personal, only from ringside as a reporter on the boxing scene. I, promoting tolerance and good will, said," Let's go to Washington, D.C. and check out the scene from the center of power."

Joe and Mike went along with it, though Mike mumbled something unprintable about New York. I had never been to Washington but looked forward to the adventure. Nothing is more fun than traveling with writers, particularly brilliant American writers.

We sat three abreast in the latest model jet run by the

Angelic Express. The trip to DC took about ninety minutes. Royko had four cocktails and a beer and was promptly entertaining all of us with stories about bumbling Chicago politicians and judges. We touched down at National Airport and within twenty minutes found ourselves outside this massive building called The Newseum.

The building was about five stories tall—all glass windows on the front. A feeling of openness and light was the effect of the architecture. Joe was the first to comment on the design, "Clever, very appropriate to the news business. Newsmen open the public's eyes to the truth in America and shed light on it."

Mike ambled ahead of us a bit. At the entrance to the museum we came upon a glass enclosed display of two dozen front pages of newspapers for the day from Maine to California. Then, all hell broke loose.

Mike yelled, "Goddamn it. What the hell did I tell you. Look at this for chrissake. This paper is a comic book, it's not a newspaper."

Joe and I caught up with him and looked down at the front page of the *Chicago Sun-Times*. The paper had a front page photo of a golf star standing at a podium looking grim. At the bottom of the page were three little graphics, one on baking, one on sports and the third on car repair. There was no writing on the front page except the headline and a sentence or two under the photos.

Joe was aghast and consoled Mike. I took it all in and attempted to process it. I found so much in my lifetime absurd. This bit of nonsense was just another chapter.

We entered the building and spent a solid five hours captivated by the history of journalism in America from penny papers to something called Internet blogging (something that

I am trying to understand).

Mike was beaming when we came upon the display of Pulitzer Prize winners. His photo was prominent for 1972, the year he won the award for Commentary. Joe had his turn at the display of press critics, where he had earned a place as the unrivaled champion.

The more time we spent in the museum, the more glum both Joe and Mike got. Joe spoke for both of them. "The news business has been captured by huge corporations. God help America in the 21st Century."

I was not as despairing as my new friends. Hope always defeats despair, always has and always will.

I lived in an earlier age and fled my native France in my middle age. At the time I fled, the country had no independent press of any kind. France had no constitution with a First Amendment like that in America guaranteeing freedom of speech and the press. My writings were smuggled into France in the early morning hours and were burned if discovered by the Catholic Church or the French government.

I felt instinctively that the need for truth and an independent press was so ingrained in the American way of government and law, that no concentration of capital could doom the news business to mediocrity and extinction.

We finished our visit to the museum and DC and were home by dinner. Royko was melancholy and very drunk by then. Joe and I got him home safely and cheered ourselves up with a great French meal and two bottles of port.

And that is the way it is.

– Voltaire

Chapter Eight: While the Democrats Slept

Forgive my foray into American history. I barely knew America before I passed into my present state: eternal satirist. But, I always thought America had great potential. Still believe that, in fact.

But, somewhere in my memory I remember a conversation with my American friend Ben Franklin. He spoke of some brilliant, courageous move by George Washington leading the American troops in ships across the Delaware River at night. The British troops were sleeping. The Americans surprised them with the nighttime attack and won a huge victory.

That is what appears to have happened this Tuesday when Republican Senatorial candidate Scott Brown upset the Democratic candidate Martha Coakley in a special election for a U.S. Senate seat from Massachusetts, a Democratic stronghold.

I just finished the *New York Times* article on the election. It appears that all the top Democrats were sleeping, vacationing, inept or some combination thereof in the lead-up to the election. Coakley, who probably would have made a fine Senator, was an inept and arrogant campaigner. In a sports-crazy state she knew little or nothing about Boston Red Sox history. She found the gritty work of politics distasteful.

The Dems in the White House (who are some of the finest

political organizers around) took Massachusetts for granted until it was too late.

I was having coffee this morning with Harry and Bess Truman, who had just finished one of their brisk walks. We were talking about the Massachusetts Senatorial election. Harry and Bess told me that Harry and his team had upset Tom Dewey in the 1948 Presidential race in a similar way. Dewey had been so far ahead in the polls in the summer of 1948 that he and his team stopped campaigning awhile until, like Coakley, it was too late.

Repeating the mistakes of the past. That is what the Democrats did on this one.

That is it for today. I am going running.

– Voltaire

Chapter Nine: College Football: A Civilizing Influence

It has been a distinct pleasure to meet so many Americans since I passed on some two-hundred-odd years ago. This rather young country seems to have such an anti-intellectual and puritanical bent to it. Witness the election of such dolts as Ronald Reagan and George W. Bush.

It seems to me that America often jolts forward toward a more humane society and then is pulled backwards just as often by the reactionaries that fool many American voters into giving them the reins of power. Such a shame. America in my view has great unrealized potential.

Forgive my digression into politics and philosophy. It comes to me as easily as breathing. And I believe Mr. Gandhi was telling me the other day that all our actions are political in some sense. He is quite right.

One very curious thing I have noticed about my American friends of the 20th century is their obsession with college football. Every Saturday I wander around my favorite haunts looking for my American friends–Mike Royko, Joseph Campbell and Brenda Ueland–only to find them obsessed with young men in helmets running in packs called the Buckeyes, Fighting Illini, Golden Bears, Thundering Herd and the Horned Frogs.

Try as I might to engage my dear American friends in just a few minutes of rich intellectual discourse on Saturdays, I always fail.

Despairing in my loneliness last Saturday I unloaded on Mike Royko (one of the funniest Americans) my disappointment in the Americans' obsession with college football. He told it to me straight: "Voltaire, get over it. If we didn't have college football and pro football on weekends, we would be wreaking a lot more havoc on the world. Not a good thing."

Mike always makes a lot of sense, I have found. And even better, he makes me laugh.

– Voltaire

ESSAYS

Michael & Anita Katsaros

Chapter Ten: The Lovers Who Started It All

The Chicago Shakespeare Theatre Company staged a wonderfully funny musical spoof of Shakespeare's *Romeo and Juliet* in the summers of 2004 and 2005. I saw the show four times and found the satire and humor in it brilliant. I still carry the musical score with me on my iPod Nano to dip into during a morning run.

A lovely, haunting love song can be found in the score of that show: "The Ones Who Started It All." In it, Romeo and Juliet lovingly tell each other that their devotion to each other kindled and bested all the great romances in history. I don't care if the exaggeration in the lyrics is belied by history. It is a great love song. If you are in love with someone, play this song for them. You will laugh and then reflect on the great gift you have been given.

That brings me to my focus today: the lovers who started it all for me—my devoted parents, Michael and Anita Katsaros. I was fortunate to have Mom's company for twenty-seven years until her premature death in 1977 at the age of 57. Dad stayed with me longer, dying when I was forty-one in 1991.

My parents were Chicagoans of Greek ancestry. I was raised to be proud of that rich and wise heritage. My lifetime of learning has shown me why.

My father was born in 1908 in Tripolis, Greece, a city of 20,000 in the mountains ninety miles south of Athens. He was the youngest of five children.

Dad emigrated to the United States in 1920 following the death of his parents. He left Greece to escape poverty and a war-torn Europe. His sister, Thea Pitsa, married and raised her family in Tripolis. Dad's brothers, George, James and Alex, emigrated to the U.S., settled in Chicago and then sent for him.

My mother was born on the south side of Chicago in 1920. She was the eldest daughter of Peter and Angeline Speropulos. Mom had two brothers and one sister. She attended Chicago public schools where she excelled.

Mom and Dad met through a Greek matchmaker, one of my father's friends. They were married at St.. Constantine and Helen Greek Orthodox Church in Chicago in 1945. I found them to be devoted to each other and their two sons throughout their long marriage. My brother Dean and I were raised in grand style with constant love, encouragement, laughter and all the creature comforts our parents could muster.

My mother and father taught us to love family and friends with the greatest devotion, sacrifice and fidelity; to value a superior education; to work hard and to fight hard. They also taught us to save money because another Depression, like the Great Depression that they starved through, was likely just around the corner.

Jack Shea, one of my favorite spiritual writers, says that if you really want to understand God, you should think of God as parental love in action. That resonates with me. I met God at birth and think of my parents with warmth and fondness every day.

Chapter Eleven: Life

Life is really a gold prospecting trip. Each day we set forth on a journey looking for gold. And most days if we are lucky we find some in loving relationships, honest creative work, families, prayer, the hopeful messages from God that come our way each day if we are awake, and in miracles (per the theologian, Jack Shea: "events and people that occur in our life that allow love to be expressed"). All these things are gold nuggets. We collect them, hold them tight; and they bring us spiritual wealth, serenity and happiness.

Today, the gold I gathered started with a delicious night's sleep, a fine prayer, feeling my body run through an eight-miler with ease while treading on a new path of snow just deep enough to give me firm footing. All my protective clothing kept me warm and cozy on a five-degree-below-zero Chicago morning.

Then, after clean-up and the donning of the crisp garb of a trial lawyer, I found a favorite seat on the Blue Line to stretch out. I jumped into a mental conversation with Ray Bradbury, who in *Zen in the Art of Writing* told me to sit down and make a list. He suggested a list of nouns and ideas from stories, childhood and life that I wanted to write about. His list, made in his tender years, gave way to nouns and then to prose essays.

A page or two into Bradbury's essays, a new character would pop into his life. He then let that character come alive and run freely, following that character into a story. The list that Bradbury started making as a youth propelled that fine soul into stories and books and plays and poems over a rewarding forty years as a writer.

I have found many gold veins in my life and mine them daily.

Chapter Twelve: Transitions Bookstore: An Appreciation

Sacred spaces are important to me. They bring serenity, hope and joy. When I leave them, I am refreshed, happy, encouraged and hopeful.

A sacred space that I treasured in Chicago for years was the Transitions Bookstore at North and Sheffield.

Walking into Transitions was like walking into your favorite church. Soothing music was always playing. Hundreds of thought provoking, nourishing books were beautifully displayed. There was a place for kids to stretch out and read with those who loved them. A café with coffee and desserts and tables for eating or writing or pondering was off to the side.

The store was a perfect place for nourishing your soul.

A couple of times I went into the store after an early Sunday Mass at Old St. Patrick's Church. The peace and serenity from the Mass continued to resonate with me as I sat on a comfortable leather bench and browsed some books on mythology or creative writing.

I rarely walked out of the store without a new book or two that fed my imagination, patted my soul on the back, beckoned the boy in me to come out and play and brought me what I valued most–courage, and its cousin, fortitude.

I bought several books on the creative process by Jane Cameron (*The Right to Write, The Sound of Paper and Walking in This World*) and a wonderful book of poetic prayers that I still read at least once a week. The book is so good that I had to make it a gift for my children and best friends that Christmas. And now my friends also read this book at least once a week.

I am not sure if my kids have opened it. Frankly, I am a little scared to ask. That is not to say that I am worried about their souls, just the breadth of their educations. But there is time for that, the oldest of the three being only thirty-two.

The *Joseph Campbell Companion* was found there. I read this book for the first time in November and December of 2005, when I was going through a transition. It was invaluable in making this unwelcome change smooth, almost seamless. Several copies of this book were purchased in 2005 for my library and as gifts to my children and friends. Two of my children have read this book and send along their endorsements (a big deal)!

Joseph Campbell was a sage. A good deal of his wisdom and insights into his fascinating life can be found in this book. Campbell out-Waldened Thoreau by several years in upstate New York during the Depression. He also hung out with the young John Steinbeck during parties and adventures when they were in their 20's. A maverick after my own heart, Campbell embraced life with the joy and enthusiasm that I have for it. He may have been the 20th century's William Blake.

Another book I discovered at Transitions is a book many writers would love, *The Book That Changed My Life* (edited by Roxanne Coady and Joy Johannessen). This book allows the reader to meet 71 fine writers through the medium of 71 short, thoughtful two-page essays. As is my habit, I have given this book as a gift once or twice to rave reviews.

Finally, I bought Ray Bradbury's *Zen in the Art of Writing* at Transitions and will forever be thankful for having that book on the shelf. The essays on the writing life in this book are so full of joy that you just want to call Bradbury up and take him out for a cup of coffee or invite him to your next writers' group meeting. Bradbury is warm and generous, a loving father and addicted to kindness.

I turned my car into the parking lot near Transitions some time ago looking forward to some time in this sacred space. I was grief-stricken (still am) to find the store dark, empty of books and in the process of being dismantled.

I am grateful for all my warm, comforting memories of this sacred space in one of Chicago's finest bookstores.

The owners of the Transitions store were deeply spiritual people and created an atmosphere of warmth, safety, happiness and hope. Beautifully done.

I really miss the joint.

* * * *

Author's Comments:

Sacred spaces are so important. I have three of them that I frequent: my Writing Room in my Victorian home, Old St. Patrick's Church, and my writing room in our Wilmette home.

From left to right: Lisa Clay, Pam Dolan, and Peter Katsaros

Chapter Thirteen: Two Redheads and a Greek

I have figured out a way to ease your guilt over not going to a worship service weekly while at the same time delivering to you the peace, reflection, joy and harmony that often comes after a religious celebration.

You guessed it—run 8 miles every Saturday morning. Even better, run it with your dear friends. Then, follow the run with fresh coffee (ambrosia for many distance runners), crumb cake, much laughter and story-telling.

For those physician friends of mine in my writers' group, (Charlie, Bud, and George) who insist that I prove everything with peer-reviewed medical journal articles, I say that the three of you should gather the statistics and write that type of article, while my running friends and I party on. My running buddies and I will be thrilled to be interviewed for your research. We promise to even shower beforehand.

I have been doing this Saturday morning 8-mile running meditation for the last 15 of my 27-year running career. It has brought me incredible joy, deep relaxation, serenity and the near-constitutional right to brag about my athletic accomplishments. And most beautiful of all the distance running has also brought me three friendships made in heaven.

I began this essay about an hour after a Saturday 8-miler.

The words leapt onto the page. This piece wrote itself. I had ever so much fun spilling my secrets.

Here are some tips on how to prepare for and enjoy a meditative run.

On Friday night you should get at least eight hours of sleep, try and stay out of the bars on Lincoln Avenue (Chicago) or Bourbon Street (New Orleans), but do consume enough alcohol to try and erase those haunting nightmares of W's eight years of shame. If the drinks don't cure the nightmares, I know some very good therapists—all of them with a sense of humor.

On Saturday morning, you should get up by six and read for at least an hour sipping coffee or some other warm drink as you dive into literature or mythology. The more fanciful the writer the better. Do not read any depressing writers like Sylvia Plath, Charles Bukowski or the collected speeches of Rod Blagojevich. Have a light breakfast—cereal, fruit or toast, perhaps some eggs. Eight miles will take you an hour to an hour and a half, or less—barring a heart attack or a bombing by Iran or Texas.

Pack some food for the journey. Your natural store of carbohydrates will exhaust itself after 55 minutes of running, and then you start to burn FAT. While burning fat to keep you going may sound like a good idea, most nutritionists for distance runners do not recommend it. So, bring along a sports bar or gel and some Gatorade for use after the first five miles.

Buy yourself a sports belt for carrying drinks and gels. Once you strap one of those on around your ample tummy or showy abs, you will immediately be recognized as a serious runner.

What about food for the mind and soul during this meditation? Well, if you are starting this run at seven a.m. in a civilized city in the Midwest, like Chicago, you can tune into a wonderful radio show on NPR—*Saturday Edition* with Scott Simon. This two hour show will take you into the news of the week, the humanities and features some great journalism by Simon and his colleagues, including the 1000-year-old, very capable Daniel Schorr (not anymore, sadly). Schorr popped up every Saturday at about eight to review the biggest news developments of the week. He was living proof that getting yourself on Richard Nixon's enemies list and following your bliss can do great things for your career and your health.

If that does not appeal to you, listen to music, or a book, or a college course on tape. I have collected about 15 college courses on tape, ranging from Shakespeare's works to Mark Twain's writing, biographies and world history. Food for your mind is never a problem. For those of you reading this, you doubtless have fertile imaginations. Those imaginations will be running as freely as you, once you are a couple of miles into your run.

NPR and some of the world's best playwrights and writers are fine companions on a long run. But, the very best way to run the 8-miler is with a running buddy. I have had three marathon running buddies over the past 15 years – all of them dear, dear people and all three of them among my very best friends. They are: Ed Shurna, Lisa Clay and Pam Dolan.

Ed Shurna and I trained and ran two Chicago Marathons together in 1998 and 1999. Those marathons were my first and second and Ed's sixth and seventh. Without him I would not have run either marathon. We had two wonderful training seasons those years, running on Saturday mornings from Dearborn Park through the near West Side (near St. Ignatius and Holy Family Church) to the lakefront running path along Lake Michigan, a circuit totalling 18 miles.

More important than the marathons was the quality of the

friendship that Ed and I forged. All the many joys and usual worries of life (plus running tips and lore) were exchanged in those long, loping training runs. We listened to each other with patience, care, and love, encouraged one another in every way possible and laughed often and much, just as Emerson recommended.

Ed is still a dedicated runner but stopped doing long distances after the 1999 Chicago Marathon. I am proud to say that we are still good friends and that our runs together were among my happiest moments ever.

Turning the pages forward to 2004, two red-headed runners—Lisa Clay and Pam Dolan—entered my life bringing me two new great friendships, as well as renewed hope and joy.

Lisa entered first during a half-marathon that we trained for in the spring of 2004. We celebrated this race along with six other runners with hamburgers and margaritas outdoors at an Irish pub near the Art Institute in late May. Lisa turned up next as a pace group leader in a marathon training group in the summer of 2004, that Pam Dolan and I joined. Pam was training for her first marathon as I trained for my third.

For sixteen weeks the three of us, along with forty other runners, met at six in the morning on Saturdays at Monroe Harbor in Chicago for the long training runs of 6-20 miles that were required to prepare for a safe marathon race. Those runs took from one to three and three-quarters of an hour. During those long runs, Pam, Lisa, and I got to know each other very well. This warm friendship of support and encouragement has kept its strength to this day.

Pam went on to run the 2004 Chicago Marathon and has done several others since—two of them with me, in 2006 and 2007. Lisa trained with us for both of those last two marathons and ran half of them with us. She has also become an outstanding yoga instructor.

Laughter ran rampant in the runs with Pam and Lisa, as did the kindness and encouragement and hope that Ed Shurna and I shared in the late '90's. Pam and Lisa and I—all three of us writers—gave our running group its name: Two Redheads and a Greek (TRAAG). Membership in TRAAG is even more exclusive than the elite membership of the Old Irving Park Literary Society.

So, if you have the endurance, I encourage you to try this 8-mile meditation weekly. I guarantee the steady running will bring you joy and serenity and, if you are lucky as me, loving friendships.

* * * *

Author's Comments:

What can I say? Distance running with saints. Such great health, such laughter, such loving care for each other over the years.

Peace and serenity comes to me with distance running and tennis. What a gift athletics has been to me. Thousands of soul-enriching runs over the last twenty-seven years brought me thousands of good ideas for loving family and friends better.

Running long gives you the time and the concentration to listen to your running friends' life stories. Listening patiently and with sympathy to another's life story is enriching to both parties. Distance runners share their lives with each other on the running path.

Healthier bodies and souls are the result.

Chapter Fourteen: A Sunday Morning in July

This Sunday started at 3:45 am. I was thrilled at the early launch.

I woke refreshed and hopeful from plenty of sleep, brewed scorching black coffee and settled in with a mythology book and a sweet biography of Molly Ivins, a progressive journalist with a lot of panache who died too young.

The day was young, just an infant. I love to start the day around four in the morning, when things are still and peaceful. The darker it is at wake-up the better. I find darkness good and welcoming. Early weekend mornings in a sacred space–my writing room–are a fertile time for my imagination. These are special times when I can unpack brilliant minds like Joseph Campbell's *The Hero With a Thousand Faces*.

Virtually every day I wake up and read for a while with some steaming coffee kicking my brain into action. My mind is perpetually curious, thirsty for more knowledge, wisdom and insights into a happy life, a good story and laughter; while my body sits patiently anticipating my morning run. I am often reminded of William Blake's words: "I have a great desire to know everything." Blake and I share a birthday and a reverence for creativity, knowledge and our fellow man.

I drink my morning coffee out of a sturdy black mug

embossed with Emerson's poem on Success. I glance at it occasionally during my morning reading and think again about the enduring wisdom in the piece. Emerson's words are also a way to center me on spiritual gifts, loves and friendships.

This morning I read about red-headed Molly Ivins, who by her early thirties had spent five years in a creative and supportive environment at *The Texas Observer*, before running into a brick wall at the *New York Times'* staid, buttoned down environment rife with office politics. The seven layers of editors in Times Square that got in the way of Ivins' voice were only tolerated by her for fourteen months before she was exiled to head the *New York Times* western bureau in Denver. She was its only writer.

Having fed body and soul on journalism, myth, and cereal, I lit out for a five mile run starting in east Wilmette, then heading south toward the Northwestern football stadium on Central Avenue in Evanston and finishing at the half-way point of Evanston Hospital at Ridge and Central. The running came easily.

A five-mile run is a special distance for me and many other runners. I can recall dozens of these runs that have brought me smiles, serenity in the face of significant losses and dozens of clever ideas and insights into happiness. I have been patient with five-milers. The bounties that have come my way usually appear in the second half of the run.

The five-miler also leaves me fully limber for longer runs of ten and fifteen miles. The first five-miler sets the stage for the perpetually easy second five-miler that may follow.

This day I put my iPod Nano aside and spent my run pondering the learning from the morning reading. Eight hours of sleep the night before guaranteed easy striding and plenty of strength.

I picked a running route that I had not followed in a while, knowing that when I got to the football stadium I would again recall the memories of the family and friends that had shared fall games with me since the fall of 1996. Those games and those loving friendships were all precious. It was good to remember each of them and important to be thankful for them.

I approached the halfway point of the run at Evanston Hospital, where my wife had received all her cancer treatments for five years. I took a break and sat on a little hill watching some light traffic head east on Central Street. A slight breeze blew around, refreshing me.

I searched for the latest *Speaking of Faith* podcast and started playing it for the run home. Krista Tippett, the moderator of the show, was interviewing Barbara Kingsolver about her book *Animal Vegetable Mineral.* Kingsolver was telling a story about learning of the harmful effects of the concentration of capital in the food industry and her attempt to educate people about the benefits of looking for locally grown foods. My oldest daughter, Sarah, had read the book and raved about it.

I was moved by Kingsolver's humanity and grateful to Tippett for hitting another home run with her radio show. This show, along with Chicago's homegrown *Wait Wait...Don't Tell Me!* and New York's *On The Media,* are my favorite NPR podcasts for my early morning runs.

By the fifth mile, I had soaked my running shirt, brought myself to the shores of a beautiful calm lake, once again put a smile on my soul and launched my imagination into recording all of this for posterity.

Life is grand.

Chapter Fifteen: The Jury Is Out

My reading this week has been typically wide-ranging and inspiring. I have been absorbed in Melvin Urofsky's well-researched biography of Louis Brandeis (an inspiring lawyer, humanitarian and U.S. Supreme Court Judge), Kevin Theis' book on his acting debut in South Florida, dips into a biography of Edward Bennett Williams (one of America's finest trial lawyers), the beginning of another blockbuster David Mamet play, "Romance," news from *The New York Times* and the occasional *New Yorker* piece.

This very morning I read some Greek mythology about why Odysseus and his crew got into trouble with the gods after the sacking of Troy. I cover a lot of ground in a week.

As Saturday dawned and time for writing came upon me, the topic that most enraged me was the retrial of Illinois' former Governor, Rod Blagojevich, his antics outside the courtroom, and the ridiculous early trial commentary of Chicago journalist Elizabeth Brackett.

Two years before Blago got indicted, it was widely known on the street in both Democratic and Republican circles in Chicago, that the Blago administration was a "pay to play" regime.

In 2010, Blago and his defense lawyers managed to fool

ONE juror of 12. This cause a mistrial on twenty counts of his federal indictment, making 2011's retrial necessary.

In the course of last year's trial, plenty of evidence emerged that Blago was a thoroughly corrupt con artist and thief. He essentially stole six years of his salary from the Illinois citizenry, doing almost no work during his time as Governor. The properly authorized tapes the FBI made of Blago's phone conversations with his staff showed him to be a foul-mouthed opportunist through and through. When the U.S. Senate seat vacated by Barack Obama's election to the Presidency opened up, Blago looked on his ability to fill that vacancy purely as an opportunity to enrich himself by trading the appointment of the seat for his economic advantage. One tape quotes Blago telling his chief of staff to make it appear that Blago was acting in the public interest during the negotiations to find him a high-paying job in exchange for the Senate appointment.

He never earned his salary as the Governor and plunged deeply into a narcissistic and grandiose lifestyle that his modest salary could not support. Spending $400,000 over a six year period on clothes for Blago and his wife, while earning a modest salary as Illinois Governor, Blago was already in deep financial trouble when the Senate appointment hit his desk.

Despite the damning evidence that emerged in the courtroom, Blago is still a free man, who loves to press the flesh before and after his days on trial, giving autographs and words of nonsensical hope to the foolish Chicagoans outside the federal courthouse on Dearborn. My God, Ben Franklin, I fear for the future of the American republic with voters like these going to the polls.

Don't get me wrong, Blago was entitled to a fair retrial and he got one before Judge Zagel and the second jury.

We are now into the seventh day of jury deliberations. A

verdict next week will probably be a win for the prosecutors and justice. Deliberations that run into a third week might signal an acquittal on many counts and a frightening acceptance of public corruption in our fair state.

* * * *

Author's Note:

The former Governor's second jury trial resulted in his conviction on seventeen felony counts. On December 6, 2011, U.S. District Judge James Zagel sentenced Blago to fourteen years in prison. Justice is Sweet.

Chapter Sixteen: Ending and Starting the Years with Loren Estleman

I like to end the year in style and start the next one with a statement about distance running, hope, and ambition.

Starting on the serene day after Christmas, when I am content knowing that I have loved my family well, I make every effort to have a hell of a lot of fun. I start by getting up as early as I can—usually in the four to four-thirty morning hour—and head downstairs to get lost in the world of crime fiction.

Jump starting my heart before my morning run with a cup of hot coffee, I nest in the stuffed chair next to the Christmas tree. Sitting next to this brightly lit ornamental history of the family, I greet a Loren Estleman novel and enter the world of crime.

Estleman has taken me into a trance like few other writers have. In a few pages I find myself in Detroit two generations ago as mobsters make their fortunes running rum and other spirits across frozen Lake Superior from Canada. What fun. What a contrast to the strait-laced, buttoned down world of law that I live in year after year.

Estleman writes with an affection for Detroit from its zenith to its decline and despair. He is also a gun expert. His descriptions reveal one who has studied them through and through and used them for recreation.

I admire Estelman's writing for its humor and its subtle moral lessons. An important quality in Estleman's writing, for me, is his skill in telling an absorbing story in about two hundred seventy-five pages. Time and time again over the ten or more Estleman novels I have enjoyed, Loren can finish a fine tale in under three hundred pages. Good for him and the rest of us with limited time for novels.

For me Christmas has always been about a pool of brand new books to swim in. My Godfather, Burt Mitchell–a high school history teacher–used to bring me two or three new history books each Christmas (no doubt launching me further into the humanities). My own family had started me down this fascinating road years before. I am deeply grateful to my parents for that.

My end of the year is a chance to stretch out, find stillness and serenity, say thanks and rest the body from the (cumulative) marathons I run weekly. Christmas vacation is about the "Pause" that Jack Shea has spoken about in his Advent reflections at Old St. Patrick's Church. It is a chance to reflect on my very happy life.

After six or seven mornings of this wonderful regimen, we come to New Year's Eve. For years, the most important part of the turning of the year is the New Year's Day long morning run. One such run (perhaps 2007) took place during a Norman Rockwell type snowfall of six or seven inches. I start these New Year's Day runs about seven in the morning. Chicago belongs to me and me alone. My footprints are the first in the snow. The beauty of a fresh snowfall in the wooded Irving Park neighborhood is breathtaking. And the run is usually blessed with some brilliant sunshine heralding plenty of hope for the year ahead.

One run, probably in 1999, went almost seventeen miles,

the year I was training for two marathons. It started in a light snowfall and ended almost three hours later in four inches of snow.

These two year-end traditions are among my dearest memories.

Peter Katsaros (left) and Matt Katsaros (right)

Chapter Seventeen: Loving

I don't remember the name of the place, but what happened there was so loving that it will never be forgotten. My son, Matt, deserves all the credit.

I walked upstairs to the second floor of this popular Chicago bar, a place on Sheffield between Belmont and Addison. Matt and his then-fiancée, Stacey, were experts at knowing all the trendy places in town. Still are.

I was headed for a party of friends to celebrate the upcoming marriage of Matt and Stacey. Matt's Mother, a truly outstanding woman, had died almost eight years earlier. She launched Matt on his successful journey through life with the greatest energy and dedication. Arriving when the party began, as my wonderful Greek Mother had raised me to do, I soon realized that I was the only parent there. I wondered whether I would be lonely in the hours ahead.

The room I entered was big, clean and well-lit with a bar in the back half of the room. Matt and Stacey, a couple with "movie star looks," as my dear friend Pam has said, greeted me with warm hugs.

Soon the room filled with over 75 friends, who I knew immediately to be among the most talented and attractive young people in Chicago. I knew quite a few of them through

Matt's days at St. Ignatius, his hockey career, and his fraternity life at Illinois. They were fun. They worked hard, played hard and were very dedicated to each other as friends. I always admired this group. They had a great balance in their lives and they took very good care of one another, always taking time to honor each other at important times in each others' lives.

For the entire time that I was at the party my son treated me with the greatest kindness and hospitality you could imagine. He spent all that time with me visiting with the people I knew and helping me meet all the others. I was, I realized, an honored guest. I was deeply touched and remember of that evening as a great expression of love and kindness.

As if the evening was not thrilling enough, the end of the night provided me even more joy. Toward the end of my stay, I was visiting with Matt's friend, Joe Walsh (now a successful young physician). Joe was always a young man with a fine affection for family–both his own and those of his friends. As we were exchanging stories about Matt, he told me that my son "was universally loved." I directly began orbiting the moon.

Matt is loved because he knows how to love the people in his life so well. He is a gift to all of us.

Chapter Eighteen: The Athenian Jury Trial

I must commend the Greeks—those of the Golden Age of course—for their marvelous contributions to democracy. Both the right to vote and the right to have cases decided by juries have civilized many societies ever since 500 B.C.

The juries in Athens took a while to choose and decide cases, given the fact that a jury had to have 501 members.

And the juries sometimes got it terribly wrong. The worst example of an Athenian jury going off the rails (forgive the prophetical reference to an industrial development that followed my death by 70 years) was its conviction of Socrates for "corrupting the young."

Those of you who know me and what I fought for and against with great energy during my lifetime recognize that religious hypocrisy drove me mad. Well, Socrates was convicted for supposedly corrupting the young by teaching them that they did not have to worship or honor the Olympian gods.

Socrates' jury trial was a travesty. The Olympian gods, after all, were a pack of scoundrels, whose escapades made some memorable stories and myths to entertain people for thousands of years. But, as moral examples of conducting a good honorable life, the Olympians were clueless.

Now that I think of it a bit, it occurs to me that to worship and honor the Olympians would do more to harm the moral fiber of the Athenian youth than a good talk over coffee with Socrates would have done.

Socrates taught the youth of Athens (and anyone else that would listen to him) for free, much to the chagrin and regret of his wife and children who had little to live on.

Too bad the Greeks did not have a brilliant constitution like the Americans devised, in which the First Amendment wisely protected a robust free speech, the freedom to exercise religion and kept the church and state at a respectable distance.

Of course the Americans had the benefit of 2200 years of recorded history to learn from and some brilliant founding fathers. The Americans saw the value in voting and jury trials, protecting both rights with great energy.

Wise folks, those ancient Greeks. So, too, the modern Americans who followed their example.

– Voltaire

Chapter Nineteen: A Writer's Voice

I have been taking creative writing classes, doing some writing in different genres and hanging around writers, dramatists and other artists since June of 1972. Like the rest of my life, this has been thrilling.

Often, I heard the phrase "writer's voice." The more I read, the more I write and the more I think about the most important issues in life, the easier it is for me to discern a writer's voice.

As I have described, I start almost every day during the business week with some reading at 3:45 a.m. in my writing room with a steaming cup of coffee at my side. I don't always know what I will read when I enter that room. This week I picked up Brenda Ueland's *Strength to Your Sword Arm.*

This book is a gold mine and its author a saint. Read one essay in this book and you will immediately understand the concept of a "writer's voice."

Ms. Ueland seems caught up in a friendly, warm conversation with her readers. She writes with a fine hopeful view of life that will immediately boost your spirits and bring a smile to your face.

There is no better writer's voice extant.

LETTER TO MY CHILDREN

Chapter Twenty: A Letter To My Children on Winston Churchill

Why study Winston Spencer Churchill's life? There are many good reasons. Consider these:

This man's perseverance is the perfect antidote to any despair or discouragement that may cross your path. He had a roller coaster of a political career but was able to leap over gigantic hurdles to get to the political stage as a world leader in 1940. Hundreds of millions of people on both sides of the Atlantic are better off for his leadership.

Winston was a champion of liberty and democracy. He gave people all over the world hope, inspired them and kept them free of paralyzing fear. He probably did that better than most theologians. Study his wartime speeches (collected in my library, thankfully) for inspiring calls to action.

Winston had a love affair with the English language, political debate and the British Empire. All but the Empire are thriving for his efforts.

In his youth, Winston had little love and support from his father and mother. He was a poor student before he got to Sandhurst, the British military academy. He usually finished in the bottom of his class. While he could not master the Greek and Roman classics or Latin, he was a good writer. He made his fortune as a writer of histories, biographies and reports of his military adventures.

His father, a prominent British politician who almost became Prime Minister, cruelly ridiculed him as a failure. His parents spent very little time with him before he entered school. His primary emotional support in his early years was his nanny, "Woom." His Mother (a beautiful American socialite) eventually became a big booster of his in his early 20's, helping him launch his military career and his career in journalism.

Churchill was a prolific writer who made his living from his own outstanding political skills, wits, courage and inspiring words. Though his father had been a prominent politician and was a descendant of the Duke of Marlborough, there was no family wealth for Churchill to inherit. He was entirely a self-made man.

Churchill always showed great courage as a warrior and political statesman. He stood up for his beliefs and would not compromise on the principles of freedom, democracy and the strength of the British Empire. He stuck his neck out on risky political positions, sometimes advancing his career in meteorically upward fashion and sometimes crashing to earth in near destruction. This happened several times in his life. He always rebounded from these enormous political and financial setbacks. Those comebacks each took from two to ten years. But, he "never gave in," just as he cautioned others never to do.

Churchill never compromised his beliefs, himself, or his country, regardless of how big his personal losses or rejections or how wrong-headed the leaders of his country were. In 1929, for example, he lost most of the fortune he had accumulated in some bad investments, got ousted from the leadership of his Party's Cabinet and was severely injured in an auto accident in New York City. He came back from all three losses, stronger and more determined than before. It took time but he was restored to wealth, health, and finally, at the age of 65, the leadership of Great Britain coinciding with the country's darkest days in May 1940, the first year of World War II.

For a ten year period, 1930-1940, he had been the lone voice in the British Parliament arguing for a rearmament of Britain and encouraging fierce opposition to Hitler's rise to power in Germany. He could not get the British or American national leaders to listen to him or stop the Nazi threat. It is possible that World War II could have been avoided and tens of millions of lives saved if his wise vision had been shared before the outbreak of war in September 1939.

"Great" is the only way to describe this man. He has taught us all how to lead a life of distinction.

POETRY

Chapter Twenty-One: Creation

First, God created children and was exceptionally good at it.

Then, God created women and again did a very fine job.

And then, God created men, thereby unleashing a force that could any day now destroy the beauty of all God's creation.

Just pick up any history book or rough draft of history—a newspaper—and watch men leading countries, businesses and churches into much misery and ruin and death

Or, turn to mythology—a place I always turn to first for wisdom and guidance. What do you find there? Narcissus was a man and the mental illness narcissism was aptly named for a man.

Do not despair at any of this.

Just give more and more women a chance at leadership and respectfully suggest to them that they not lead like men - world history's greatest narcissists.

PRAYERS AND MEDITATIONS

Chapter Twenty-Two: Mantras

Perhaps it is the Easter season that has brought me to such a spiritual place. It does not matter why I am at the writing table peering into the eternal; I am here and delighting once again to be writing.

Almost every day I start the day with some reading, but this week I also spent some morning reading time with my mantras. These are four dozen yellow index cards that I have been collecting for the past five years with writings and quotes that inspire me, keep hope alive and ward off despair. Here are some of them and their authors.

* * * *

"Miracles are events and people that occur in your life that allow love to be expressed."

– Jack Shea, Starlight (1992)

My life has been full of miracles.

* * * *

"God can best be understood in the love parents show for their children."

– Fr. John Cusick, excerpt from homily on Holy Thursday

I am the oldest son of two of the most loving parents that ever walked this earth.

* * * *

"For I know the plans I have for you, declares the Lord, plans to prosper you and not harm you, plans to give you hope and a future."

– Jeremiah 29:11-12

* * * *

"The most certain sign of wisdom is cheerfulness."

– Michel deMontaigne

BOOK REVIEWS

Chapter Twenty-Three: Review of The Watchman by Robert Crais

Robert Crais and I met through his early novels in November of 2009. I was trying a five week case before two of the worst judges in the Circuit Court of Cook County (names withheld until they get indicted). I therefore had only about twenty minutes each morning over my cup of coffee to do some reading. Two of Crais' novels became my morning diet. The high quality of Crais' writing and his exotic imagination was a welcome contrast to the mediocrity of so-called justice that my clients and my trial partner were suffering through.

Instantly, I became a big fan of Crais and have now read five of his novels, the most recent being, *The Watchman*. After hitting four home runs with the first four, Crais' *Watchman* was a barely a double.

I was used to being led through a fine crime tale by Crais' narrator, Elvis Cole, a funny, yoga-practicing, gourmet-cooking sleuth. Cole heads a two person L.A. detective firm bearing his name. He has such a great sense of humor—even during some perilous times—that it is perhaps too fanciful to believe. I have chosen to believe it anyway, because I always pick hilarity over grief. Always have and always will.

Besides his humor, Cole is endearing in other ways. He falls in love, not often, but when the right woman shows up;

enjoys mornings (as I do), is loyal to his friends, is very, very tough, and shoots well.

Elvis' partner in the firm is Joe Pike. Crais tells us early in this novel that a pike is a "long-bodied, predatory fish known for its speed and aggression." (It also happens to be the nickname for my fraternity, Pi Kappa Alpha, but there is no reason to go there).

Joe Pike is a taciturn ex-Marine known for his warning: "I am coming in." That usually means that Pike is leaving the management of his two gun stores to come to Cole's aid. It also guarantees that one or more criminals are about to be gunned down with amazing precision.

So, I sat down with *The Watchman* expecting to be entertained by Elvin Cole and got Joe Pike as narrator instead. Crais gave plenty of warning. The cover of the novel describes it as "a Joe Pike novel." I chose to ignore the warning because Cole was such a charming character.

The plot of the story centers around a Paris Hilton type, Larkin Barkley, who happens to be on the hit list of some mobsters from Colombia, Ecuador and perhaps the Middle East. In the course of guarding Larkin from a sixth assassination attempt, Crais provides some background as to why Pike is a man of few words and no longer a L.A. cop. Grim stories both.

The novel picks up some speed and, importantly, humor in the middle, when–you guessed it–Elvis Cole comes on to help his buddy. More drama, another lying lawyer giving the profession a bad name, plenty of gunshots. Anymore, I cannot say without ruining the fine ending.

Four out of five novels by Crais have been so well done. That is an .800 batting average. A winning percentage like that can only be maintained if Cole leads the way.

Chapter Twenty-Four: Review of Basket Case by Carl Hiaasen

This is a funny pot-boiler that I recommend. Though it is not as good as some of this fine novelist's other books, you may enjoy it. I got the book as a gift and enjoyed it while I ran some morning miles.

Carl Hiaasen's hero, Jack Tagger, is a charming investigative journalist with too big a mouth (I can relate to him. I was born with the same defect). Tagger was knocked off his hard-won perch as a newspaper's chief investigative reporter after his public denunciation of his boss, Race Maggot III, the Rupert Murdoch-type owner of a Florida daily paper.

Tagger has been exiled to the obit column for the past two years. Most recently he has been bothered by his young editor, Emma, an attractive, smart woman twenty years his junior. This Generation X'er and Tagger have been fighting with each other.

When Tagger's research into the untimely death of a famous singer leads him right into the middle of a murder investigation involving the dead singer's wife and many semi-illiterates populating the rock music production world (some would say the underworld), Tagger and Emma find their relationship changing.

Blind ambition and greed ruined Macbeth, Nixon, untold

others and were also the undoing of Hiaasen's murderer in this tale.

Chapter Twenty-Five: Review of The Girl Who Kicked the Hornet's Nest by Stieg Larsson

My lovely, devoted partner, Joanne Medak, got me to the end of this suspenseful novel about evil, investigative journalism, and superbly talented women with guts and sex appeal. My thanks to you Joanne.

A year ago I read two hundred pages of this book and hit a wall, returning the book to Joanne. Reading long novels of almost six hundred pages, Stieg Larsson's typical length, happens occasionally in my voracious reading life but not often. I have many exciting reasons for the frequent interruptions in my novel reading, which make longer novels difficult, but will leave them for other essays and conversations.

About a year after falling off the ramparts of this imposing novel, the third of the trilogy by Stieg Larsson, Joanne encouraged me to try again. The stars were all in alignment this time. In fact, I was about to see many stars. We were on the eve of our summer vacation to the Colorado Rockies. I had plenty of time to read, the Medak's quiet Colorado home to stretch out in, and my ever hungry imagination to cut loose. I got into the flow of the book the second time around and finished it satisfied.

The novel is focused on the dire plight of the diminutive computer genius hacker and Terminator-like crime fighter,

Lisbeth Salander. Salander is near death as the book opens, having been shot twice by her father, the dreadful Zalachenko. He was a Russian defector to the Swedish spy agency in the 60's, whose criminal ways—brutal wife-beating being a prominent horrific example—have been covered up by a rogue group of spies working illegally in Sweden's CIA, the SIS.

Salander has a boatload of problems. Most threatening is the bullet lodged in her brain, followed closely by an eight count criminal indictment that would keep her in jail for many years if the charges were proven.

This is a complex novel told by a master storyteller. The themes in this novel should be thought provoking to 21st century Americans. Let us turn to some of them.

One question that may haunt the reader as she winds her way through this book is: how many computer hackers are there like Salander and her Trinity group (some of the good guys and gals), who are so skilled at hacking that the email and work product files of Salander's chief prosecutor, international security firm heads and people like you and me are readily accessible ? It is enough to birth nightmares about the hazards of paying bills online.

An important theme of this and the other novels in the trilogy is that women are still being treated very badly by men in power. Salander, you learn, has been victimized by her Father, her brother, a corrupt sadistic psychiatrist, a dozen or more Swedish spies and a lawyer, who masqueraded as her legal guardian. The bad guys are *all* guys.

Erica Berger, an outstanding magazine publisher featured in the book, runs into a brick wall of conniving, male deputy editors when she takes over as the Editor in Chief of Stockholm's largest daily newspaper. She encounters another major problem along the way—a male stalker who through the theft of some confidential photos threatens to harm her reputation on the Internet.

Fortunately for the male sex (in general), there are some men in this novel that go through life with courage and integrity, a respect for truth, the law and justice. Michael Blomkvist, a successful investigative journalist of Woodward and Bernstein's caliber, is dedicated to unearthing the truth about Salander's mistreatment and the corruption in the Swedish spy agency. Following Blomkvist through this trilogy is great fun. His creative work and tenacity will either thrill you for the first time or rejuvenate your interest in the importance of investigative journalism in societies throughout the world. Other men representing their gender well, including the lawyer director of the Committee for Constitutional Protection, the judge in the Salander criminal trial and some policemen, joined with Blomkvist in the pursuit of justice.

While on the investigative journalism point: upon reading the book, ask yourself, what magazines in the United States resemble Larsson's fictional *Millennium*, the magazine equivalent of *The Washington Post* in Watergate days. I am not sure of the answer and am troubled when a nominee does not pop into my brainpan immediately .

Stieg Larsson concludes his short-lived novelist career as a brilliant story-teller in weaving this complex plot, made more complex by scores of Swedish names and locations. Larsson is adept at frequently changing scenes, building momentum and suspense, and providing plenty of startling action. If you need a detective story fix of shootings, high drama, plenty of corpses, intrigue and really bad guys, this long book will delight you.

As if all that drama and intrigue were not enough, the scenes of the Salander criminal trial warmed my heart and displayed my profession of trial-lawyering as the dignified calling it is. The disrobing and demolition of a corrupt psychiatrist by Salander's defense attorney was authentic and exciting. It showed once again that "cross-examination is the greatest engine of truth."

Edward Burke said that "evil only prevails if enough good men do nothing." In Larsson's 21st century world there is plenty of evil. Wretched, grisly acts abound. The evil is found in affirmative acts and acts of indifference. Fortunately, Salander and some very courageous people fought like hell for her against gargantuan obstacles. The unfolding of justice in this long tale was frankly, beautiful. It was also vaguely reminiscent of the long journey America successfully traveled in its Watergate days.

www.ingramcontent.com/pod-product-compliance
Lightning Source LLC
Chambersburg PA
CBHW021121130626
46554CB00002B/802

* 9 7 8 0 9 8 3 8 8 4 6 0 6 *